I Am So Lost

Level 5 – Green

Helpful Hints for Reading at Home

The graphemes (written letters) and phonemes (units of sound) used throughout this series are aligned with Letters and Sounds. This offers a consistent approach to learning whether reading at home or in the classroom.

HERE IS A LIST OF NEW GRAPHEMES FOR THIS PHASE OF LEARNING. AN EXAMPLE OF THE PRONUNCIATION CAN BE FOUND IN BRACKETS.

Phase 5			
ay (day)	ou (out)	ie (tie)	ea (eat)
oy (boy)	ir (girl)	ue (blue)	aw (saw)
wh (when)	ph (photo)	ew (new)	oe (toe)
au (Paul)	a_e (make)	e_e (these)	i_e (like)
o_e (home)	u_e (rule)		

HERE ARE SOME WORDS WHICH YOUR CHILD MAY FIND TRICKY.

Phase 5 Tricky Words			
oh	their	people	Mr
Mrs	looked	called	asked
could			

GPC focus: /oy/ir/ay/ea/

TOP TIPS FOR HELPING YOUR CHILD TO READ:

- Allow children time to break down unfamiliar words into units of sound and then encourage children to string these sounds together to create the word.
- Encourage your child to point out any focus phonics when they are used.
- Read through the book more than once to grow confidence.
- Ask simple questions about the text to assess understanding.
- Encourage children to use illustrations as prompts.

This book focuses on the phonemes /oy/, /ir/, /ay/ and /ea/ and is a green level 5 book band.

I Am So Lost

Written by
John Wood

Illustrated by
Steph Burkett

Elroy is off to visit Gran. Elroy stops at the end of the street. Is it left, or right?

"Left is the way to Gran," says Elroy.
"I am sure."
Elroy turns left. He cannot wait to see
Gran.

This part of town is odd. The roads are green, and it smells of eggs. Elroy turns left again.

Is this the way to Gran? Elroy is not so sure, but he plods on.

Elroy has not seen this part of town. It is full of clocks, and the girls and boys have hats on.

Now Elroy is not sure if this is the way to Gran.
"I might be lost," says Elroy.

Now Elroy starts to float up and up and up. He is trapped in the strings of a hot air balloon!

"Oh no," says Elroy. "This is not the right way."
"Hang on!" yells the man in the hot air balloon.

Elroy lands in a big tree. He sits still. He can hear the sounds of animals nearby.

A frog hops near.
"I am so lost," says Elroy.
The frog croaks in a sad way. Elroy sets off.

Elroy is at the top of a hill. Elroy is not sure how he has got so lost.

The wind is loud and strong.
"You are not Gran," says Elroy.
The goat snorts and licks Elroy's cheek.

Oh dear. Elroy is in the sea.
He sees a squid. The squid might tell him the way to Gran.

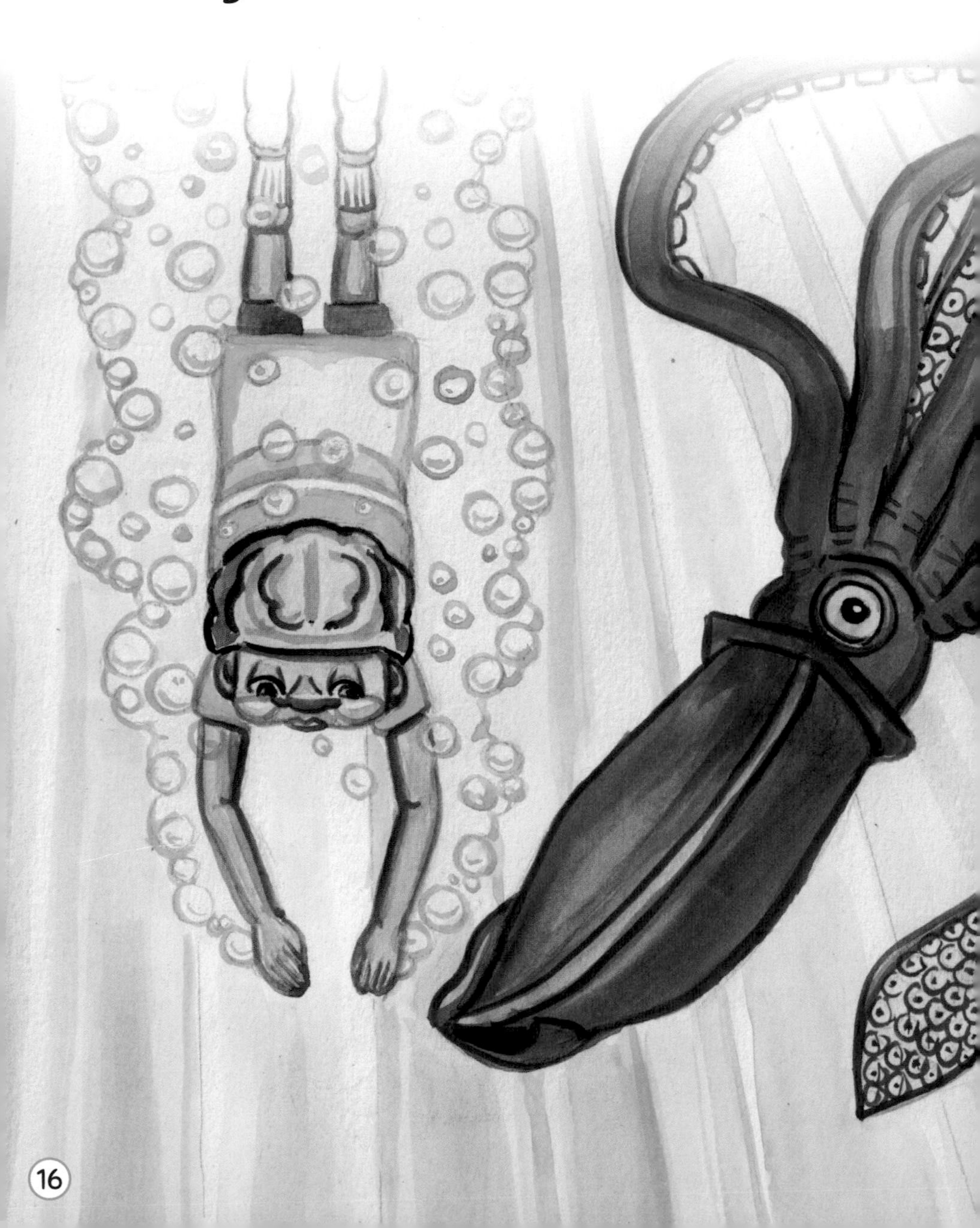

Elroy taps the squid. But the squid shoots out ink and swims away!
"I am so lost," thinks Elroy.

Now Elroy is on a beach. There is sand in his socks and seaweed in his hair.

"Have you seen Gran?" Elroy says to a bird.
The bird chirps and flaps its wings.

"As long as I do not stop, I will get to Gran," says Elroy.
But Elroy steps too far and falls off the planet.

"This is not good," says Elroy. "This is not good at all."
The ground is far away now.

Elroy floats far away into the black night. The stars glint and the Moon gleams.

There is no sound. There is no wind.
"I am so lost," says Elroy into the dark.

Look! It is Gran in a ship.
"How did you get so lost?" yells Gran.
"Did you turn right?"

"No, I went left," says Elroy.
"Oh dear, Elroy. Quick, get in the ship," she says.

"You found me!" says Elroy. "But Gran, how did you hear that I was so lost?"

Gran turns and points to the back of the ship.
"With their help," she says.

Look! It is the man in the balloon, the frog, the goat, the squid and the bird.

"Thank you!" says Elroy, as he hugs them all. "It feels good to be found."
"Let's go back," says Gran.

I Am So Lost

1) Did Elroy turn left or right?

2) Where did Elroy land after floating in the hot air balloon?

3) What animal did Elroy meet at the top of the hill?

a) Tiger

b) Bat

c) Goat

4) Where did Gran find Elroy?

5) Have you ever been lost? What would you do if you were lost?

©2021 **BookLife Publishing Ltd.**
King's Lynn, Norfolk PE30 4LS

ISBN 978-1-83927-404-6

A catalogue record for this book is available from the British Library.

I Am So Lost
Written by John Wood
Illustrated by Steph Burkett

An Introduction to BookLife Readers...

Our Readers have been specifically created in line with the London Institute of Education's approach to book banding and are phonetically decodable and ordered to support each phase of Letters and Sounds.

Each book has been created to provide the best possible reading and learning experience. Our aim is to share our love of books with children, providing both emerging readers and prolific page-turners with beautiful books that are guaranteed to provoke interest and learning, regardless of ability.

BOOK BAND GRADED using the Institute of Education's approach to levelling.

PHONETICALLY DECODABLE supporting each phase of Letters and Sounds.

EXERCISES AND QUESTIONS to offer reinforcement and to ascertain comprehension.

BEAUTIFULLY ILLUSTRATED to inspire and provoke engagement, providing a variety of styles for the reader to enjoy whilst reading through the series.

AUTHOR INSIGHT:
JOHN WOOD

An incredibly creative and talented author, John Wood has written about 60 books for BookLife Publishing. Born in Warwickshire, he graduated with a BA in English Literature and English Language from De Montfort University. During his studies, he learned about literature, styles of language, linguistic relativism, and psycholinguistics, which is the study of the effects of language on the brain. Thanks to his learnings, John successfully uses words that captivate and resonate with children and that will be sure to make them retain information. His stories are entertaining, memorable, and extremely fun to read.

This book focuses on the phonemes /oy/, /ir/, /ay/ and /ea/ and is a green level 5 book band.